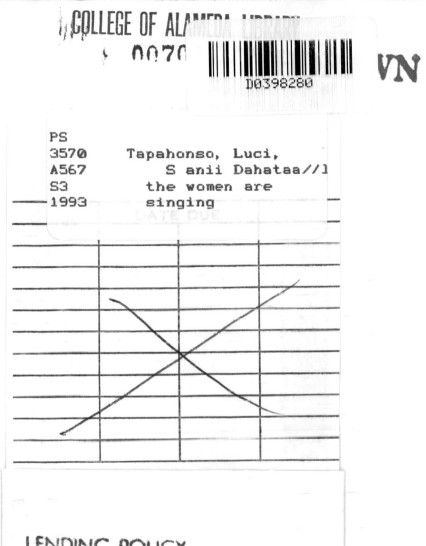

Sáanii Dahataał

The Women Are Singing

Volume 23
SUN TRACKS
An American Indian Literary Series

Series Editors
Ofelia Zepeda and Larry Evers

Editorial Committee
Vine Deloria, Jr.
Joy Harjo
N. Scott Momaday
Emory Sekaquaptewa
Leslie Marmon Silko

Sáanii Dahataał
The Women Are Singing

POEMS AND STORIES

Luci Tapahonso

The University of Arizona Press · Tucson & London

The University of Arizona Press
Copyright © 1993
Luci Tapahonso
All Rights Reserved

♾ This book is printed on acid-free, archival-quality paper.
Manufactured in the United States of America.

98   97   96   95   94   93   6   5   4   3   2   1

Library of Congress Cataloging-in-Publication Data

Tapahonso, Luci, 1953–
    Sáanii Dahataał, the women are singing : poems and stories / Luci
Tapahonso.
        p.   cm. — (Sun tracks ; v. 23)
    ISBN 0-8165-1351-1. — ISBN 0-8165-1361-9 (pbk.)
    1. Navajo Indians—Literary collections.   I. Title.   II. Series.
PS3570.A567S23   1993   92-35093
811′.54—dc20   CIP

British Library Cataloguing-in-Publication Data
A catalogue record for this book is available from the British Library.

For Bob G. Martin

whose love for late night stories

sustains both of us

Contents

Preface: The Kaw River Rushes Westward

North of our home in Lawrence, Kansas, the Kaw River flows wide and brown. When I first saw this river, I was surprised at how deep and how loud it is. Its banks are lined with thick groves of trees. In comparison, the San Juan and Rio Grande rivers in New Mexico are clear and shallow. One fall we drove home to Shiprock, New Mexico, about 1300 miles away. Our route took us across Kansas, into Colorado, and then down into northwestern New Mexico. It was such a contrast to see the wide fierce water change to the quiet shallow San Juan in New Mexico. The terrain in Kansas is mostly rolling hills and flat plains, and as the rivers changed, the landscape did also, ranging from steep canyons, mountain gorges, and finally emptying out into the Rio Grande riverbed. This flowed into the San Juan, which is a mile south of my parents' home. The night we arrived in Shiprock I was very much aware that the river nearby was quiet, reflecting the dark sky and stars above. Alongside this river are huge, old cottonwoods; willows and tamarack brushes are tucked along the sandy cliffs.

We drove into the yard late at night and my parents were awake, waiting for us. After we ate a long-awaited meal of mutton stew and náneeskaadí, tortillas, we went to bed. It was dark and quiet in the house of my childhood. My daughter and I talked quietly awhile before we fell asleep. In the darkness, we heard the faint songs of the Yeis, the grandfathers of the holy people, and the low, even rhythm of the drum. They had been dancing and singing for six days and nights already. From across the river valley, the songs drifted into our last waking moments, into our dreams. While we slept, they sang, praying and giving thanks for the harvest, for our return and the hundreds of others who returned home that weekend for the fall festivities. The Yeis danced for all of us—they danced in their fatigue, they danced in our tired dreams. They sang for us until their voices were hardly more than a whisper. Around three the next morning, they stopped to rest.

In the morning, we woke refreshed and happy. The morning air was clear and crisp with a harvest chill, and there across the blue valley stood Shiprock, a deep purple monolith. I drank coffee outside, watched the dogs act silly, and then I caught up on news of what had happened since my last trip. While we ate breakfast, my father watched news, the table radio played Navajo and English songs alternately, my mother told me a little story about when she was four or five years old, I braided my daughter's hair, and two of my sisters came over to visit. This is the familiar comfort I felt as a child, and it is the same for my children. The songs the Yeibicheii sang, that the radio played, and that my mother hummed as she cooked are a part of our memories, of our names, and of our laughter. The stories I heard that weekend were not very different from the stories I heard as a child. They involved my family's memories, something that happened last week, and maybe news of high school friends. Sometimes they were told entirely in Navajo and other times in a mixture of Navajo and English.

There is such a love of stories among Navajo people that it seems each time a group of more than two gather, the dialogue eventually evolves into sharing stories and memories, laughing, and teasing. To be included in this is a distinct way of showing affection and appreciation for each other. So it is true that daily conversations strengthen us as do the old stories of our ancestors that have been told since the beginning of the Navajo time.

Just as the rivers we followed home evolved from the huge, wide Missouri River to the shallow water in the San Juan riverbed, the place of my birth is the source of the writing presented here. This work ranges from stories I heard as a child, to stories that were told by relatives, friends, or colleagues, and to other poems and stories that are based on actual events. Most of the pieces originated in Navajo, either

orally or in thought, and the English translation appears here. I have
retained the first person narrative in most of the stories because it is
the stronger voice and truer to the person who told the story origi-
nally. Many of these poems and stories have a song that accompa-
nies the work. Because these songs are in Navajo, a written version
is not possible. When I read these in public, the song is also a part
of the reading. This is very much a consideration as I am translating
and writing—the fact that the written version must stand on its own,
even though I know that it is the song which makes it complete.

The combination of song, prayer, and poetry is a natural form
of expression for many Navajo people. A person who is able to
"talk beautifully" is well thought of and considered wealthy. To
know stories, remember stories, and to retell them well is to have
been "raised right"; the family of such an individual is also held in
high esteem. The value of the spoken word is not diminished, even
with the influences of television, radio, and video. Indeed, it seems
to have enriched the verbal dexterity of colloquial language, as for
instance, in the names given to objects for which a Navajo word does
not exist, such as "béésh nitséskees" or "thinking metal" for compu-
ters and "chidí bijéí" or "the car's heart" for a car battery.

I feel fortunate to have access to two, sometimes three languages,
to have been taught the "correct" ways to use these languages, and to
have the support of my family and relatives. Like many Navajos, I was
taught that the way one talks and conducts oneself is a direct reflection
of the people who raised her or him. People are known then by their
use of language.

It is with this perspective that I share the following stories, poetry,
and prayers. Once my oldest brother said about my nálí, my paternal
grandmother, who died decades ago: "She was a walking storybook.
She was full of wisdom." Like many other relatives, she had a profound

understanding of the function of language. This writing, then, is not "mine," but a collection of many voices that range from centuries ago and continue into the future.

For many people in my situation, residing away from my homeland, writing is the means for returning, rejuvenation, and for restoring our spirits to the state of "hohzo," or beauty, which is the basis of Navajo philosophy. It is a small part of the "real thing," and it is utilitarian, but as Navajo culture changes, we adapt accordingly.

I view this book as a gift from my mother and father, both of whom embody the essence of Navajo elders—patience, wisdom, humor, and courage. It is a collaboration of sorts with my sisters and brothers, my extended family, and my friends. I especially appreciate the tremendous support of my daughters and my husband. Their thoughts, humor, and encouragement sustain me and all I undertake. Ahéhee'.

Sáanii Dahataał

The Women Are Singing

Blue Horses Rush In

For Chamisa Bah Edmo,
who was born March 6, 1991

Before the birth, she moved and pushed inside her mother.
Her heart pounded quickly and we recognized the sound of horses running:

> the thundering of hooves on the desert floor.

Her mother clenched her fists and gasped.
She moans ageless pain and pushes: This is it!

Chamisa slips out, glistening wet and takes her first breath.
> The wind outside swirls small leaves
> and branches in the dark.
Her father's eyes are wet with gratitude.
He prays and watches both mother and baby—stunned.

This baby arrived amid a herd of horses,
> horses of different colors.

White horses ride in on the breath of the wind.
White horses from the west
where plants of golden chamisa shimmer in the moonlight.

She arrived amid a herd of horses.
Yellow horses enter from the east
bringing the scent of prairie grasses from the small hills outside.

She arrived amid a herd of horses.

Blue horses rush in, snorting from the desert in the south.
It is possible to see across the entire valley to Niist'áá from Tó.
Bah, from here your grandmothers went to war long ago.

She arrived amid a herd of horses.

Black horses came from the north.
They are the lush summers of Montana and still white winters of Idaho.

Chamisa, Chamisa Bah. It is all this that you are.
You will grow: laughing, crying,
and we will celebrate each change you live.

You will grow strong like the horses of your past.
You will grow strong like the horses of your birth.

The Weekend Is Over

The weekend is over and we have to leave.
My throat is so heavy, I can hardly swallow.
My daughters' smiles are quivering at the edges.
Their eyes glisten.

"Well, I guess we'll go now," I say.
Everyone has gathered around. My mother and sisters
hold the girls, saying, "Do good in school, baby,
don't forget to pray, be good to yourself, shiyázhí."
My father tells them, "Take care of your mother."
My brother says, "Tell Bob to come next time.
All us Navajos won't hurt him." We laugh.
The girls are saying, "Bye, Grandma. Auntie, auntie, bye."
"See you," they wave at the kids playing under the trees.
Bah runs over and asks, "Are you guys going now?
I thought you were going back tomorrow. It's NOT fair,"
she says, her lower lip stuck out. We hug her and say,
"We'll come back again pretty soon."
"Bye Grandma. Hógoónee' Shicheii. Bye Cherie."
I hold baby Fred one more time. We always say
that even at a year old, he already has a cowboy look.
"Hágoónee', shiálchíní," my mother says. "Goodbye, my children."
I hug my father lightly. His shoulders are thin and warm.

Finally, we drive away and everyone is watching and waving.
There must be about forty people there
and that's not even half of our family.

They are all smiling, and suddenly, I notice
we all look so much the same: slightly slanted eyes,
ready smiles, and black, dark hair.

Before we leave Shiprock, we make one last stop
and I buy coffee brewed over an open fire
and mutton and green chile wrapped in warm tortillas for all of us.
Lori buys a thick slice of Navajo cake—sweet blue corn squares.
The girls stay awake until we leave our home country—Dinetah.

Then they fall asleep for the next two days of driving.
The car hums over smooth roads.

"The land of Kansas," I say aloud to no one in particular.

Just Past Shiprock

When I was a child, our family traveled often to Oak Springs, Arizona. Oak Springs is on the eastern slope of the Carriso Mountains, about fifty miles west of Shiprock. My father grew up there, and we have many relatives in the area. Our family has a plot of land with a hogan and storage cellar there.

On one occasion, we were going to Oak Springs, and there were perhaps six or seven children in the back of the pickup and Mary, an older cousin. Mary's father and my mother are siblings, so she is considered our sister. She is considerably older than we are and did not take part in the noisy playing we were involved in. Since she was the oldest one in the back of the pickup, she was responsible for our behavior or misbehavior.

As we went past Shiprock, there were flat mesas, gentle sandhills, and a few houses scattered at distances. Mary pointed to a mesa as we rounded a curve and asked, "See those rocks at the bottom?" We stopped playing and moved around her to listen. The question was the opening for a story. The rocks she pointed at were midway between the ground and the top of the rock pile. The mesa loomed behind, smooth and deep ochre. The rocks were on the shaded side of the mesa. Then Mary told this story:

They said a long time ago, something happened where those rocks are. When I was little, they told me that one time before there were cars or even roads around here, there was a family traveling through here on horseback. They had a little baby girl who was sick. As they came near here, the baby became sicker, and she kept getting worse. They finally stopped. They knew it was no use going on. They just stopped and held the baby. By then, she was hardly breathing, and then finally she just stopped breathing. They just cried and walked around with her.

In those days, people were buried differently. The mother and father wrapped her in a pelt of sheepskin and looked for a place to bury her. They prayed, sang a song, then put the baby inside. They stacked rocks over this place so that the animals wouldn't bother her. Of course, they were crying as they rode home.

Later on, whenever they passed by those rocks, they would say, "Our baby daughter is right there," or "She would have been an older sister now." They wiped their tears, remembering her. A lot of people knew that the baby was buried there—that she was their baby and that they still missed her. They knew that and thought of the baby as they passed through here.

So that's why when we come through here, remember those rocks and the baby who was buried there. She was just a newborn. Think about her and be quiet. Those rocks might look like any others, but they're special.

We listened to the story, and since that time we have told the story many times ourselves. Decades later, those particular rocks hold the haunting and lasting memory of a little baby girl. This land that may seem arid and forlorn to the newcomer is full of stories which hold the spirits of the people, those who live here today and those who lived centuries and other worlds ago. The nondescript rocks are not that at all, but rather a lasting and loving tribute to the death of a baby and the continuing memory of her family.

In 1864

In 1864, 8,354 Navajos were forced to walk from Dinetah to
Bosque Redondo in southern New Mexico, a distance of three
hundred miles. They were held for four years until the U.S.
government declared the assimilation attempt a failure. More
than 2,500 died of smallpox and other illnesses, depression,
severe weather conditions, and starvation. The survivors
returned to Dinetah* in June of 1868.

While the younger daughter slept, she dreamt of mountains,
the wide blue sky above, and friends laughing.

We talked as the day wore on. The stories and highway beneath
became a steady hum. The center lines were a blurred guide.
As we neared the turn to Fort Sumner,† I remembered this story:

A few winters ago, he worked as an electrician on a crew
installing power lines on the western plains of New Mexico.
He stayed in his pickup camper, which was connected to a generator.
The crew parked their trucks together and built a fire in the center.
The nights were cold and there weren't any trees to break the wind.
It snowed off and on, a quiet, still blanket. The land was like
he had imagined from the old stories—flat and dotted with shrubs.
The arroyos and washes cut through the soft dirt.
They were unsuspectingly deep.
During the day, the work was hard and the men were exhausted.
In the evenings, some went into the nearby town to eat and drink
a few beers. He fixed a small meal for himself and tried to relax.
Then at night, he heard cries and moans carried by the wind
and blowing snow. He heard the voices wavering and rising

---

* "Dinetah" means "Navajo country" or "homeland of The People."
† Fort Sumner was also called "Bosque Redondo" owing to its location.

in the darkness. He would turn over and pray, humming songs
he remembered from his childhood. The songs returned to him
as easily as if he had heard them that very afternoon.
He sang for himself, his family, and the people whose spirits
lingered on the plains, in the arroyos, and in the old windswept plants.
No one else heard the thin wailing.
After the third night, he unhooked his camper, signed his time card,
and started the drive north to home. He told the guys,
"Sure, the money's good. But I miss my kids and it sure gets lonely
out here for a family man." He couldn't stay there any longer.
The place contained the pain and cries of his relatives,
the confused and battered spirits of his own existence.

After we stopped for a Coke and chips, the storytelling resumed:

My aunt always started the story saying, "You are here
because of what happened to your great-grandmother long ago."

They began rounding up the people in the fall.
Some were lured into surrendering by offers of food, clothes,
and livestock. So many of us were starving and suffering
that year because the bilagáana* kept attacking us.
Kit Carson and his army had burned all the fields,
and they killed our sheep right in front of us.
We couldn't believe it. I covered my face and cried.
All my life, we had sheep. They were like our family.
It was then I knew our lives were in great danger.

* "Bilagáana" is the Navajo word for Anglos.

8

We were all so afraid of that man, Redshirt,* and his army.
Some people hid in the foothills of the Chuska Mountains
and in Canyon de Chelly. Our family talked it over,
and we decided to go to this place. What would our lives
be like without sheep, crops, and land? At least, we thought
we would be safe from gunfire and our family would not starve.

The journey began, and the soldiers were all around us.
All of us walked, some carried babies. Little children and the elderly
stayed in the middle of the group. We walked steadily each day,
stopping only when the soldiers wanted to eat or rest.
We talked among ourselves and cried quietly.
We didn't know how far it was or even where we were going.
All that was certain was that we were leaving Dinetah, our home.
As the days went by, we grew more tired, and soon,
the journey was difficult for all of us, even the military.
And it was they who thought all this up.

We had such a long distance to cover.
Some old people fell behind, and they wouldn't let us go back to help them.
It was the saddest thing to see—my heart hurts so to remember that.
Two women were near the time of the births of their babies,
and they had a hard time keeping up with the rest.
Some army men pulled them behind a huge rock, and we screamed out loud
when we heard the gunshots. The women didn't make a sound,
but we cried out loud for them and their babies.
I felt then that I would not live through everything.

* Kit Carson's name was "Redshirt" in Navajo.

9

When we crossed the Rio Grande, many people drowned.
We didn't know how to swim—there was hardly any water deep enough
to swim in at home. Some babies, children, and some of the older men
and women were swept away by the river current.
We must not ever forget their screams and the last we saw of them—
hands, a leg, or strands of hair floating.

There were many who died on the way to Hwééldi.* All the way
we told each other, "We will be strong as long as we are together."
I think that was what kept us alive. We believed in ourselves
and the old stories that the holy people had given us.
"This is why," she would say to us. "This is why we are here.
Because our grandparents prayed and grieved for us."

The car hums steadily, and my daughter is crying softly.
Tears stream down her face. She cannot speak. Then I tell her that
it was at Bosque Redondo the people learned to use flour and now
fry bread is considered to be the "traditional" Navajo bread.
It was there that we acquired a deep appreciation for strong coffee.
The women began to make long, tiered calico skirts
and fine velvet shirts for the men. They decorated their dark velvet
blouses with silver dimes, nickels, and quarters.
They had no use for money then.
It is always something to see—silver flashing in the sun
against dark velvet and black, black hair.

* Hwééldi is the Navajo name for Fort Sumner.

They Were Alone in the Winter

Each night, I braid my daughter's hair.
My fingers slip through the thick silkiness,
weaving the strands into a single black stream.

"The air feels like something will happen,"
she says. "Maybe it will snow."
The moon outside is a silver arc in the cold sky.
"In the old stories, they say the moon comes as a beautiful horse,"
I tell her. From the bedroom window, we look out

           at the glistening night sky.

It is outside the house: the frozen night.
It glimmers with her pleas for snow.
It glimmers in her night dreams: a fusing of music, laughter,

           talk of boys and clothes.
It glimmers here in the fibers of my bed sheets,

      there above the old roar of the Kaw River.
It glimmers in the western sky where he thinks of me and smiles.

In an old story, a woman and her daughter were alone in the winter
and the mother said, "Tomorrow, if the sun rises,

        it will come as many different horses."

They Are Silent and Quick

We sit outside on the deck
and below, tiny flickers of light appear here and there.
They are silent and quick.
The night is thick and the air alive with buzzing and humming insects.
"They're lightning bugs," Lori says. "Fireflies."

I wonder how I will get through another day.

"I think that they are connected with magic," she says,
peering into the darkness. "Maybe people around here tell stories
about small bits of magic that appear on summer nights."
"Yes," I say, "it must be."

I walk inside the house and phone my mother.
From far away, she says, "I never heard of such a thing.
There's nothing like that in Navajo stories."
She is speaking from hundreds of miles away
where the night is dark and the sky, a huge, empty blackness.
The long shadows of the mesas stretch across the flat land.
"Someone is having a sing near here," she says. "We can hear
the drums all night long. Your father and I are all alone here."
Her voice is the language of my dreams.
I hang up the phone and walk out into the moist air.

My daughter sits there in the darkness, marveling at the little beings
filled with light, and I sit beside her.
I am hoping for a deep restful sleep.
In the woods below, teenagers are laughing
and the whine of the cicadas rises loudly.

"What is it?" she asks. "What's wrong?"

There are no English words to describe this feeling.

"T'áá 'iighisíí biniinaa shil hóyéé'," I say.

> Because of it, I am overshadowed by aching.

> It is a heaviness that surrounds me completely.

"Áko ayóó shil hóyéé'." We are silent.

Early the next morning, I awaken from a heavy, dreamless sleep
and outside the window, a small flash of light flickers off and on.
Then I recalled being taught to go outside in the gray dawn
before sunrise to receive the blessings of the gentle spirits
who gathered around our home. Go out, we were told,
get your blessings for the day.

And now, as I watch these tiny bodies of light,
the aching inside lessens as I see how
the magic of these lights precedes the gray dawn.

It Was a Special Treat

Trips to Farmington were a special treat when we were children. Sometimes when we didn't get to go along, we cried so hard that we finally had to draw straws to decide fairly who would get to go. My oldest brother always went because he drove, my other brother went because he helped carry laundry, my father went because he was the father, and my mother went because she had the money and knew where to go and what to buy. And only one or two kids were allowed to go because we got in the way and begged for things all the time.

We got up early on the Saturdays that we were going to town—we would get ready, sort laundry, and gather up pop bottles that we turned in for money. My father always checked the oil and tires on the pickup, and then he and my brothers would load the big laundry tubs, securing the canvas covers with heavy wooden blocks. We would drive out of the front yard, and the unfortunate ones who had to stay home waved good-bye sullenly. The dogs chased the truck down the road a ways before turning home.

In Farmington, we would go to the laundry first. It was always dark and clammy inside. We liked pulling the clothes out of the wringer even though my mother was nervous about letting us help. After that, we drove downtown and parked in the free lot north of Main Street. Sometimes my father got off at the library, and we picked him up after we finished shopping. Someone always had to "watch" the pickup, and usually the one who was naughty at the laundry had to sit in the pickup for two or three hours while everyone else got to "see things" around town. If my father didn't go to the library, the kids were off the hook, naughty or not, because he waited in the pickup and read "The Readers Digest."

When we stopped at Safeway, our last stop, it was early evening. My mother would buy some bologna or cooked chicken in plastic wrapped trays and a loaf of bread. We would eat this on our way home. After the groceries were packed in securely under the canvas and wooden blocks, we talked about who we saw, what we should have bought instead of what we did buy (maybe we could exchange it next time), then the talking would slow down and by the time we reached the Blue Window gas station, everyone but my father was sleepy.

He would start singing in Navajo in a clear, strong voice and once in a while, my mother would ask him about a certain song she heard once. "Do you know it? It was something like this . . ." and she would sing a bit, he would catch it and finish the song. We listened half asleep. I would whisper to my sister, "He sounds like those men on Navajo Hour." "I know. It's so good," she'd answer, and we'd sleep until we reached home.

It Has Always Been This Way

For Lori and Willie Edmo

Being born is not the beginning.
Life begins months before the time of birth.

Inside the mother, the baby floats in warm fluid,
and she is careful not to go near noisy or evil places.
She will not cut meat or take part in the killing of food.
Navajo babies were always protected in these ways.

The baby is born and cries out loud,
and the mother murmurs and nurtures the baby.
A pinch of pollen on the baby's tongue
for strong lungs and steady growth.
The belly button dries and falls off.
It is buried near the house so the child
will always return home and help the mother.
It has been this way for centuries among us.

Much care is taken to shape the baby's head well
and to talk and sing to the baby softly in the right way.
It has been this way for centuries among us.

The baby laughs aloud and it is celebrated with rock salt,
lots of food, and relatives laughing.
Everyone passes the baby around.
This is so the child will always be generous,
     will always be surrounded by happiness,
and will always be surrounded by lots of relatives.
It has been this way for centuries among us.

The child starts school and leaves with a pinch of pollen
on top of her head and on her tongue.
This is done so the child will think clearly,
listen quietly, and learn well away from home.
The child leaves home with prayers and good thoughts.
It has been this way for centuries among us.

This is how we were raised.
We were raised with care and attention
because it has always been this way.
It has worked well for centuries.

> You are here.
> Your parents are here.
> Your relatives are here.
> We are all here together.

It is all this: the care, the prayers, songs,
and our own lives as Navajos we carry with us all the time.
It has been this way for centuries among us.
It has been this way for centuries among us.

Sháá Áko Dahjiníłeh
Remember the Things They Told Us

1

Before this world existed, the holy people made themselves visible
by becoming the clouds, sun, moon, trees, bodies of water, thunder,
rain, snow, and other aspects of this world we live in. That way,
they said, we would never be alone. So it is possible to talk to them
and pray, no matter where we are and how we feel. Biyázhí daniidlí,
we are their little ones.

2

Since the beginning, the people have gone outdoors at dawn to pray.
The morning light, adinídíín, represents knowledge and mental awareness.
With the dawn come the holy ones who bring blessings and daily gifts,
because they are grateful when we remember them.

3

When you were born and took your first breath, different colors
and different kinds of wind entered through your fingertips
and the whorl on top of your head. Within us, as we breathe,
are the light breezes that cool a summer afternoon,
within us the tumbling winds that precede rain,
within us sheets of hard-thundering rain,
within us dust-filled layers of wind that sweep in from the mountains,
within us gentle night flutters that lull us to sleep.
To see this, blow on your hand now.
Each sound we make evokes the power of these winds
and we are, at once, gentle and powerful.

4

Think about good things when preparing meals. It is much more than
physical nourishment. The way the cook (or cooks) think and feel become
a part of the meal. Food that is prepared with careful thought,
contentment, and good memories tastes so good and nurtures the mind
and spirit, as well as the body. Once my mother chased me out of the kitchen
because it is disheartening to think of eating something cooked
by an angry person.

5

Be careful not to let your children sit or play on tables or countertops.
Not only is it bad manners, but they might have to get married
far sooner than you would ever want.

6

Don't cut your own hair or anyone else's after dark. There are things
that come with the darkness that we have no control over. It's not
clear why this rule exists, but so far no one is willing to become
the example of what happens to someone who doesn't abide by it.

Leda and the Cowboy

A few months back, when the night sky was darker
than Leda had ever seen, she stepped through
the worn door frame of the Q lounge.
The suddenness of thick smoky air left her slightly faint.
After that, it was easy enough, Leda saw him across
the damp just-wiped bar—she did nothing
but hold the glance a second too long.
Sure enough, as if she had called out his name,
he walked over   a slight smile and straw hat.

Even then, as they danced, the things he told her
were fleeting. Leda smiled and a strange desperation
engulfed him. "I have to leave," she said,
remembering the clean, empty air outside.
He followed her, holding her shoulder lightly,
and outside, he bent over: his body an arc in the street light,
and it was clear he didn't know the raw music she lived.

But for now, he is leaning across the table, smiling,
and telling Leda things: he wants to take her on a picnic,
                    it might rain tonight,
                    and she can phone him anytime.
He thinks he is leaving for a rodeo 400 miles to the north
in a few hours. His pickup is loaded with saddles, clothes,
and a huge ice chest. Leda notices the parking lot outside
is stained with oil, twisted cigarettes, and small bits of
colored glass. He leans toward her, hat tilted, and in that
low morning voice says he has been tracking her all night.

In this desert city of half a million people, he drove
over cooled asphalt trails searching smoky dance halls,
small Indian bars, the good Mexican place that serves
until 11, and when he found her at a table near
the dance floor, she was laughing. But Leda saw his
straw hat and half-smile as he watched from the bar.
When they danced, it was flawless.
He thinks he has done this many times before.
His shirt carried the scent of the hot night breezes outside.

East of here, above the dry fields of the Hoohookamki,
the stars are sparse, and as he follows Leda through
the stark beauty of the old stories,

he has already left his own life behind.

These Long Drives

between Cuba or Grants
fall short of the usual comfort.

My younger brother, shisíli,
made a beaded ring for me—yellow daisies with black centers.
He was a rough-and-tumble third grader
and I was in high school: intent on being the best western stomp dancer,
and maybe snagging a tall Chinle cowboy.

Years later, his interest in mechanical objects
kept my car running well. On trips home from various cities,
he filled the tank, rotated the tires, and changed the oil
as easily as I changed boots. After each visit, I left assured
my car would run another 5,000 miles or so. At any hint of car trouble,
I rushed home to my younger brother while my car could still make it.

This brother died at 22. One day he was
driving his trusty old pickup, laughing
and joking. Then he turned silent,
a thin figure beneath hospital sheets.
His slow death entered my blood.
I breathe it with every step.

The middle brother is a few years older than I.
He is a father, master mechanic, and stern uncle.

Once when I was at his home, his little son came inside
and whispered into his shoulder, "Daddy, the rabbit won't talk."
My brother laughed and hugged his son.

"The Volkswagen won't start," he told us.
He held his son a while, then they walked over to fix the stalled car.

His sons will grow up to be good cooks and fine mechanics.
They will care and abide by the wishes of the women
in their lives as my brother does.

> Sometimes he curses the long desert miles between us
> when he senses I may be in danger. This city protects crazed men
> who are freer than I. My brother finds ways to console my anguish
> and fear over distances of telephone wire and urgent visits
> to medicine men. His steady voice calms me on dark evenings.

My oldest brother: such vivid images I have of him.
He Tarzan-like and I a skinny, dark child swinging on his arms.
He was tall and girls giggled around him. We wondered why
they called him then turned silly at his approach.

> He was killed by a preacher's son, and at 13 years old
> I was stunned to find the world didn't value
> strong, older brothers and that preaching
> the gospel life could be nothing.

I am remembering my brothers tonight
and during a strange spring snowstorm, my mother calls
and tells me about some little thing she remembered from years ago.

Laughing into the phone, I see outside the wonderful snow,
                    seemingly endless, warm and cold at once.

No one could have predicted this storm.

It is all strange, beautiful, and we will talk of this
for years to come. This storm, and I will think of how

how I missed my brothers just then.

Hills Brothers Coffee

My uncle is a small man.
In Navajo, we call him, "shidá'í,"
         my mother's brother.

He doesn't know English,
         but his name in the white way is Tom Jim.
         He lives about a mile or so
         down the road from our house.

One morning he sat in the kitchen,
drinking coffee.
         I just came over, he said.
         The store is where I'm going to.

He tells me about how my mother seems to be gone
every time he comes over.
         Maybe she sees me coming
         then runs and jumps in her car
         and speeds away!
         he says smiling.

We both laugh—just to think of my mother
jumping in her car and speeding.

I pour him more coffee
and he spoons in sugar and cream
until it looks almost like a chocolate shake.
Then he sees the coffee can.

Oh, that's that coffee with the man in a dress,
like a church man.
Ah-h, that's the one that does it for me.
Very good coffee.

I sit down again and he tells me,
        Some coffee has no kick.
        But this one is the one.
        It does it good for me.

I pour us both a cup
and while we wait for my mother,
his eyes crinkle with the smile and he says,
        Yes, ah yes. This is the very one
        (putting in more sugar and cream).

So I usually buy Hills Brothers Coffee.
Once or sometimes twice a day,
I drink a hot coffee and

        it sure does it for me.

One Dog Story

They say that Navajos shouldn't buy or sell dogs because they are con-
sidered family members. This means, too, that dogs are expected to
be responsible and to possess some degree of intelligence. At times,
my father owned dogs who understood only Navajo and would extend
their right paw when someone said "Yá'át'ééh" to them. We told my
father that, rather than dog obedience school, his dogs would have to
enroll in bilingual education classes so they could learn English, too.
Sometimes people criticize pets saying, "I don't know what's wrong
with that dog. He has no respect! Doesn't even listen! Just runs into
the house all the time!" Likewise, a well-behaved dog earns affection
and respect quickly. Generally, dogs are valued as sheepherders, watch
dogs, and playmates for the children.

Once at my mother's home, I was told this story:

This family in Shiprock farm area was without pets for a few weeks,
which was unusual, because most Navajo homes have at least four
or five dogs around. It seemed that where the family lived, there was
someone or something going around stealing pets from people. Both
cats and dogs, they said. The whole situation was very strange, and
it was all everyone talked about. Of course, everyone was suspicious
and on the lookout constantly. Every unfamiliar car in the area was
watched closely. They figured it had to be bill collectors or animal
stealers. There was even some talk of devil worshipers and satanic
cults, but that was too much to imagine. Most families just knew that
their pets were quite handsome and therefore irresistible to anyone
looking for a dog or cat.

One day, Angie was unloading her car. She had just driven back from work at Cudei when a blue GMC pickup drove up. A woman leaned out and asked, "Are you people missing a dog?"

"Yeah," she said, putting everything down.

"Well, I know where your little dog is," she said, "but first, don't ask me my name, or where I'm from."

"Okay," Angie said, growing more excited by the minute.

"There's a woman by the last name of Tso who lives at Ojo Amarillo. She's the one that stole your dog. Just the little one. She's sure bragging around about it up there at Ojo Amarillo, telling everyone she stole a good Doberman from your family. So if you guys want your dog, that's where it is," she said. "That Tso lady is my sister-in-law and we don't get along. That's why I told you," she added, then drove quickly out of the yard.

Their mother said that after that "crimestopper" came, everyone in the family found out about what she said. They were out to find that Tso lady. She was suspected of stealing more than the dog. One of the other sisters, who lives at Ojo Amarillo, which is a mutual-help housing project, heard about all this that very evening. Right away she found out where that woman lived. She called a Navajo Police officer for help—he had also been asking her out. He said (in his official capacity), "I'll help you recover your parents' dog."

That night around nine, the officers and Angie's sister went to the suspect's house and a man answered the door. Upon seeing her angry sister and the law, he said, "Go 'head. Go on back to the yard and get the dog." Some kids watched quietly as they walked through the house to the backdoor. There was no sign of the offending dognapper—that Tso lady. But at least they located the dog and took it. Angie's sister was sure glad she has some influence with the law enforcement.

That same night, after 10:30 P.M., she and her kids arrived at their parents' home, some twenty-five miles away. "Who's that? so late," her mother mumbled, looking out the front window.

"Mom, we have something for you and Dad," Angie's sister said, lifting up the dog for her to see. Everyone was happy and they all settled into the kitchen. They told about how they found the Tso lady and how they confiscated the dog with the help of the law. By now, another sister came over from next door and her brother drove in to hear the whole story. Finally, they all had to leave. The kids had school the next day. That night, they went to bed happy. At least we have one dog back, they said several times to each other.

The next day Joe, another dog, came home. Joe had also been missing and then just appeared on the porch in the morning. They guessed he had just run off—he wasn't the type to get stolen. He came back even more skinny and raggedy than before. Once their mother went out on the porch and yelled real loud, "Yo! Joe!" And everyone looked at each other in surprise. They thought only Marines and miners yelled "Yo!" to answer roll call or the phone. And here she was yelling that to Joe! After that, sometimes the aunts (some of whom had been to boarding school) called "Joe Babe!" to him and then just about fell over laughing when he came running. Joe Babes were girls at boarding school who teased their hair, wore lots of mascara, and wore white go-go boots when that was the style. They said they could tell Joe wasn't a boarding school product!

Two days after Joe came back, Angie's mother called one of her other daughters, Becky, who had given her Dale, the puppy who had been stolen and then returned. She asked, "Did Dale have his ears pinned?"

"Yes," her daughter answered. There was silence for a while.

"Was his tail cut?" her mother asked.

"Yes," she said. "I have the rest of it over here." Becky lives on the other side of the Chuska Mountains, about eighty miles away.

"Hmm . . . ," her mother continued. "Was Dale a boy dog?"

"Chip and Dale are both boys," Becky answered. Chip was Dale's brother and she had kept Chip for her own pet.

"Oh dear," her mother said. "Your sister brought the wrong dog back to me. This one's ears just flop around and it has a long tail. Joe's been acting like Dale's a female. Oh dear. I guess he has a wife now."

The last we heard, Joe was happy with Dale or whoever they thought Dale was. They just kept calling her "Dale," since they remembered that Roy Rogers had a wife named Dale.

Dít'óódí

For Bob

The skin behind one's ear is exquisite: thin, delicate
         dít'óódí   dít'óódí

I hear words from your mouth,
    wet and warm with breath.

    It is said that the wind enters each newborn,
    a whoosh of breath inside, and the baby gasps.
    It is wet with wind. It is holy. It is sacred.
    Such energy we are, with wind inside.
        alive   alive

Tell me words from the warmth of your mouth, throat
down to darkness of heart beating, beating
    it travels then to my ears
    skin surrounding it
        dít'óódí   dít'óódí
            cradling the pulse.

    My pulse: mirror of heart
    gentle, steady organ
    swaying in red warmth inside me
    inside me: all that ever ached,
        all I have cried about,
        all I have laughed through.

Tell me words of healing,
    words of holiness.
        Utter slowly into these wires of magic,
        900 miles shimmering with care and tears.

My doctor said: Take these every day. The only effect
        may be a slowed heartbeat.

It is so.
Speak to me words.
My heart quickens a bit, reaching back into recent days, last month
for pulses missed, skipped over as I slept in darkness.
My heart beats slower, slower.
Two beats slide into one.

I sleep on. A dream scene is much too slow
but anything can happen in dreams.
    Later as I walk down the aisle, selecting cuts of meat,
    in between picking up something tasty and easy to fix
    and a roast to simmer all day;
    steam rising, warm and spicy from the oven,
    my pulse slowed. It remains there,
    beating above shiny tile and chilled air:
        a small space of loneliness.

Your voice retrieves the missing pulses of my heart.
It works. It works over distances of hills, flat plains,
    lonely silos, and sturdy houses of the Midwest
    and I am healed.

Your breath of words secure beneath
the solid white bone around my ear
and my pulse continues steadily.
Your words, your life swirls inside
the dark depths of my own body.

It Is a Simple Story

She appeared to us on a cold January morning
in Liberal, Kansas:
> that small misnamed motel town.
> Dorothy and cohorts smile frozen,
> north of highway 54 awaiting yet another tornado
> in the yard of the famous white frame house.

Perhaps the woman who appeared to us in room #124
died from an overdose of pills and sweet red wine.
Maybe she drifted off to death after a fight
with the lover who betrayed her.
She remains there, wearing a long nightgown,
clutching her forehead and pacing across the room.
She moves slowly from the door to the bathroom,
a sad, floating form.

She appeared a little after 3 A.M. as we slept.
We were harmless enough: a tired mother, two energetic daughters,
> and two nervous cats.

We understood why she appeared to us and were not frightened.
What did we know of her life or her death? we asked each other.
We felt the quiet loneliness in the bend of her shoulders,
the dull ache in the sides of her head,
and the emptiness in her heart spilled out into the room.
The next morning, we drove away from the slow heaviness of her walk
and into the brightness of the highway stretching across Kansas.

Many months later, we drive into a small valley,
east of Wichita and the Flint Hills are soft
in the November sunset. The grasses undulate sleek gold.

We pull off the highway and walk around,
encircled by the curving hills.
I want to remember this: the huge, pink sun in the pale sky
and my husband's face as he looks out across the hills—

       somewhere deer are sniffing the air,

       recognizing our scent.
I want to remember this: Misty's hair shining in the still air.

            She smiles quickly, easily, then turns.

These hills surround us in all shades of brown and gray.
It is in this calmness, in the pale sky above,
and in the wind grazing at our clothes and hair
that I feel the quiet loneliness of the dead in this vast place,
and I know that we are with them,

           together and apart.

She Says

The cool October night, and his tall gray hat
throws sharp shadows on the ground.
Somewhere west of the black volcanoes,
dogs are barking at something no one else can see.

His voice a white cloud,
plumes of chimney smoke suspended in the dark.

Later we are dancing in the living room,
his hand warm on the small of my back.
It is music that doesn't change.

The ground outside is frozen,
trees glisten with moon frost.

The night is a careful abandonment of other voices,
his girlfriend's outburst brimming at the edge of the morning,

and I think I have aged so.
His warm hands and my own laugh are all we share in this other life
strung together by missing years and dry desert evenings.

Tomorrow the thin ice on black weeds will shimmer in the sun,
and the horses wait for him.
At his house around noon, thin strands of icicles drop
to the ground in silence.

Early Saturday, the appaloosa runs free near Moenkopi.
The dog yips, yips alongside.

Raisin Eyes

I saw my friend Ella
with a tall cowboy at the store
the other day in Shiprock.

Later, I asked her,
Who's that guy anyway?

Oh, Luci, she said (I knew what was coming),
it's terrible. He lives with me
and my money and my car.
But just for a while.
He's in AIRCA and rodeos a lot.
        And I still work.

This rodeo business is getting to me, you know,
and I'm going to leave him.
Because I think all this I'm doing now
will pay off better somewhere else,
but I just stay with him and it's hard
because

        he just smiles that way, you know,
        and then I end up paying entry fees
        and putting shiny Tony Lamas on lay-away again.
        It's not hard.

But he doesn't know when
I'll leave him and I'll drive across the flat desert
from Red Valley in blue morning light
straight to Shiprock so easily.

And anyway, my car is already used
to humming a mourning song with Gary Stewart,
complaining again of aching and breaking,
down-and-out love affairs.

Damn.
These Navajo cowboys with raisin eyes
and pointed boots are just bad news,
but it's so hard to remember that all the time,
she said with a little laugh.

How She Was Given Her Name

One cold winter afternoon,
the baby ran outside when no one was looking.
She ran, laughing, and waving her arms around.

"The baby!" someone yelled and we ran out after her.
She heard us and ran even faster,
down the sloping hill to the orchard.
We could hear her laughing and squealing.
The dogs were bounding alongside her in the snow.

Finally, she was caught, and when they brought her inside,
she was still laughing, her cheeks and arms red.
She was just happy, breathing hard, and eyes sparkling.
She hadn't been outside all winter.

"She escaped," my brother said.

After that time, she tried to run outside when she thought
no one was watching, and she ran for the road each time.

So her name became "Beep-beep"
because she liked to be a roadrunner
and she liked having people try to catch her.

If Shiyázhí Could Speak

That dog outside with the curled-up tail and bright hungry eyes has
quite a history. His name is Shiyázhí, which means my little one in
Navajo. He is a friendly and handsome dog.

One day when we came home, he was missing. Maybe he was stolen,
lured with a bit of meat (he is always hungry), or maybe he squeezed
through the little opening in the gate (for a chubby dog, he could fit
almost anywhere). That evening, there was no welcoming reception,
no wild barking and loud panting, no jumping at the door and then on
us, no licking and generally behaving as if we'd been gone for weeks
rather than just the day. Once you are welcomed home in that way,
nothing else will do. That evening, there was only silence. No response
to "Shiyázhí, where's Mommy's baby boy?" Instead, there were only
empty, overturned bowls in the messy yard. The backyard was silent,
scattered with ragged dog toys, and the gate was open.

Bob drove slowly around the neighborhood and I walked along the
streets calling Shiyázhí. We were out until almost midnight. Misty
stayed home, looking out the windows and pacing the front yard. She
thought he might get tired and come home.

The next morning we placed boxes that yelled in huge letters:
REWARD! LOST DOG! REWARD! on several street corners. We pinned Shi-
yázhí's picture to several reward posters at the grocery stores and told
the neighbors of our plight. We placed ads in the newspapers among
other desperate pleas for lost pets. Our ad was distinctive and different
because it was for Shiyázhí. REWARD, it read in bold capital letters. We
didn't speak of how much we would actually pay; we knew we would
pay any amount to have him back.

A week went by and the backyard stayed achingly clean. His bowls
were stacked neatly, and the patio door was still smeared with nose
and paw prints. The cats became more sociable—regaining control of

the house—and they dared to sit on the back porch for long periods of time.

Then two weeks later, on a Sunday morning, a woman called saying, "I saw the ad about your dog and I think I know where he is." She told of a woman named Rosie, who was keeping a Norwegian elkhound in Algodones, a small village alongside the river some twenty miles north of Albuquerque. Rosie didn't have a phone and the caller did not want to give Rosie's last name.

Armed with that information, Bob took several recent pictures of Shiyázhí and drove to Algodones to begin going from house to house, starting at the point where the phone lines ended. He showed Shiyázhí's picture, asking, "Have you seen this dog?" At one house, a little boy who was interpreting for his grandfather said, "Yes, my grandpa saw a dog like that back there at that house." At the house they pointed out, a woman said, "No, I haven't seen him, but he sure is a pretty dog." Bob asked if she knew someone named Rosie who lived somewhere around there. She knew her and pointed to a mobile home further north and said, "Rosie lives there, but don't tell her I told you. She's my daughter." And although she told Bob where Shiyázhí was, she refused to take any reward money.

So that's where Shiyázhí was, in Algodones with a woman named Rosie. Rosie said Shiyázhí was with a man from northern New Mexico who was selling apples beside highway 44. The dog jumped out of his truck, she said, and wouldn't go back to the apple man. When Shiyázhí saw Bob, he was overjoyed, jumping and yelping, that Rosie was just happy to see them back together. "Just take your poor dog," she said. "Look how he missed you." She had forgotten that she wanted to keep Shiyázhí for herself. She, too, would not let Bob give her any reward money.

On the way home, Bob stopped at a roadside stand to buy chile and the people there said, "Is that your dog? A man who sells apples is looking for a dog like that."

Bob showed them the pictures in his shirt pocket and said, "This is my dog. I just got him back."

"I guess that is his dog—has pictures and everything," they said among themselves.

Shiyázhí came home and ran immediately to eat the cats' food, and the cats ran to hide, horrified that he was home. We hugged him and laughed, almost crying. He thumped his tail on the floor and licked our arms, hands, and faces. "We have a second chance now," Misty said, "a second chance with Shiyázhí."

The yard was messy again and we were greeted to no end each day when we returned home. That Shiyázhí has quite a history and if he could tell us his part of the story, we would be even more amazed that he is home. But for now, we tell our story, and people say, "It's a miracle you got him back." After all, he could have been a traveling apple salesdog. At Easter, we went back to Rosie's house with a basket and Shiyázhí. She was surprised at how much he had grown. Shiyázhí was happy and seemed to smile at her from the back seat.

Light a Candle

For Hector Torres

The other night thunder shook the house
and lightning slashed brilliant blue across the bed.
I slept in bits, my heart raced with each explosion of noise and rain.
And though he held me, my breathing was ragged and exhausted.
I may never sleep through these storms.

Hector, light a candle for me.

Last week we returned to our birth place,
and as we drove through southern Colorado,
we were stunned by the beauty of autumn leaves,
the deep cool mountain canyons,
and twice, deer stood beside the road.
They watched as we passed through their land.
Their eyes glistened black softness.
Misty said, "Isn't it neat that we saw them on our way home?"

Hector, light a candle for her.

In a small reservation town, a little boy shakes his mother.
She has passed out on the floor and he is hungry.
"Mama," he says, "can you make some potatoes?"
She stirs, "Leave me alone, damn it!"
He climbs up on the counter, takes down a box of Cheerios
and sits back down to watch TV.
The noise he makes eating dry cereal is steady and quiet.

Hector, light a candle for him.

Some evenings Leona just wants to sit with her sisters and mother
around the kitchen table and talk of everything and nothing.
Instead, she sits in the quiet kitchen, and outside
leaves blow against the window—the wind is cold and damp.
In front of Leona, the table stretches out clean and shiny.

Hector, light a candle for her.

North of here, the Kaw rushes westward, a wide muted roar.
The trees alongside sway and brush against each other,
dry, thin leaves swirl in the cold wind.
The river smell and heavy wind settle in my hair,
absorbing the dull thundering water,
        the rolling waves of prairie wind.

This time I have walked among the holy people:
the river, the wind, the air swirling down from the hills,
the exhilaration of the biggest catch,
the smooth grace of eagles as they snatch their prey,
the silent pleas of those who drowned here.

Hector, light a candle for me.
        Light a candle for me.

What Danger We Court

For Marie

Sister, sister,
what danger we court
without even knowing it.
It's as simple as meeting a handsome man for lunch at midnight.

Last Friday night
at the only stop sign for miles around,
your pickup was hit from behind.
That noise of shattering glass behind your head,
whirl of lights and metal as two cars hit your pickup—
that silent frenzy by tons of metal spinning you
echoes the desert left voiceless.

Sister, sister,
what promises they must be for you
when you walk the edges of cliffs
sheer drops like 400 feet—
vacuums of nothing we know here.
You turn and step out of the crushed car dazed
and walk to help small crying children from another car
and you come home, sister,
> your breath intact,
> heart pounding,
> and the night is still the same.

Your children cry and cry to see you.
Walking and speaking gently,
> your voice gathers them in.

What danger we court.

It is the thin border of a miracle, sister, that you live.
The desert surrounding your house is witness
to the danger we court and

sister, we have so much faith.

The Pacific Dawn

It is spring in Hilo, Hawaii,
and the Pacific dawn is brilliant with color.
Early on, it is bright pink, streaks of gold line the clouds.

It awakens me,
drawing me to the window
to pull back drapes,
fill the entire room with the dawn.

I lie back down to sleep again.
Birds outside the window talk noisily.

I am tired. My eyes ache
and I want to sleep and sleep;
nurture my body and let my bones soak
in quiet breathing and soothing thoughts.

But it is this: the dawn and the pounding ocean below;
clouds rearranging themselves over and over.
I breathe this air, gentle with alive flowers,
and cannot sleep.

Not far from here, Pele stirs, she sighs, and it is a thick stream
of hot steam atop the dry volcano. She sees him—the dark handsome one
with a moustache. His hat is new and fine. Pele sits up and takes
a deep breath—she likes nice things. His hat blows off and whirls
downward to the center of her home. He reaches after it,
but it is lifted away. "Oh Pele," he says, smiling, "it is for you
I wore the hat."

Just yesterday, I felt her strength,
brimming beneath the molten island.
I leaned over the rim of the black volcano
and sprinkled corn pollen, whispered a prayer;

        I recall First Man and First Woman.
        I recall the first perfect ear of white corn.
        I recall the first perfect ear of yellow corn.
        I recall the dust of my desert home.

I left a Zuni bracelet; perfectly shaped turquoise stones
set in smooth white silver and earrings, long thick jaatł'óół.
She loves the most beautiful of everything.

I understand that I was destined to see this dawn,
        to say this prayer,
        and I am helpless in this beauty:

        The huge flowers I couldn't have imagined,
        the lilting songs of the throaty chanters,
        the nurturing stories of long ago,
        and those who spread luau before us
        as if we have just come home.

It is here that my dreams take on an unnameable restlessness,
and the heavy currents of the Pacific force themselves into my memory.

It Is Night in Oklahoma

The used air in a plane and the still air in a wide terminal
are no different than the vast skies shared with other silent travelers.
To most people, our leaving is nothing more than a hollow roar,
than an empty runway space.

It is night in Oklahoma when he walks toward me,
his voice low and eyes brimming from that raw place inside.
His brother's death is a jagged sigh flooding him:

>   It has taken him back to his birth,
>   the first faces he knew: Mother and Tommy.
>   The long humid afternoons of his boyhood,
>   trapping crawdads and playing baseball swept over him.
>   How sad the dirt-stained pants,
>   the old TV shows flicker black and white.
>   The days of high school are framed with longing.

Now on long football afternoons, his step will waver
when he gets up to call his brother, then remembers.
He will walk nearer me as we journey through music-filled stores,
all around us glistening tinsel and forced cheer.

>   There are no words for this anguish.
>   His brother is dead.

From the airport, I drive back through
the dark frozen streets, squeezing his hand.
He sits beside me, his breath ragged wet.
We cross the black yard, slick with ice, and enter the house.
My steps are small and frightened.

Inside we circle the rooms with corn pollen,
sprinkling old words, sprinkling old pleas for help and wholeness:
>   Nihi Diyin, nihíká iilyeed.
>   Nihíká iilyeed, nihi Diyin.
We move the furniture around,
straighten the rooms as his people have always done.
These rooms gather us in, yet hold the empty space left by death.

Later he holds me in the darkness.
He holds me, breathing into my hair.
>   My hair: thawed from the iced night air
>   and damp with exhausted sighs.
>   As his smooth hands slide down my back and legs,
>   I suddenly feel drunk, but then I recognize
>   the frightening dizziness that grief causes.

Slowly, slowly we move into each other,
>   that warm, familiar slickness.
>   It seems all that we have in the torn winter ahead.

In other rooms, perhaps troubled spirits hover in the dark air,
above the same old furniture, above sleeping limp bodies, and
above the covered pans of food on the counters.
>   But in here, we breathe each other's skin,
>   move to feel our pulses beating,
>   and this is the only reassurance of
>   our own tender lives,
>   our own tender lives.

Outside a Small House

Somewhere in the north valley
outside a small house,
moths flutter powder wings
against the gleaming windows.
The windows: clear panes of death.

Inside, he paces back and forth
then slams his fist into the wall.
His buddies look up startled, then resume talking.
They are used to this: his days and nights
                    are tireless blurs of stories and poetry,
                    careful arrangements and rearrangements
                    of words and pauses that erupt
                    as full breathing memories.

No one has called me at 3 A.M. in the last ten years,
but tonight the phone rings and I am confused.

        "Can you talk?" he asks.
        He is trapped by an old loneliness—
        an old longing to hear a soft voice
        tell him stories he's never heard.
        I listen to his urgency and imagine his knuckles
        starting to bruise: first, a burning red, then light blue.
        By sunrise, dark purple circles of blood
        brimming beneath taut skin.
        I tell him the bruises will heal in about a week.
        The healing will be a reversal of colors:

purple, blue, dim red, finally yellow.

Then there will be no traces.

But for now, the moths outside the windows fall slowly.

They will lie soft and silent in the dawn.

Shúúh Ahdę́ę

We call him "Shúúh" because he is always ready to hear a story. When we're in a noisy restaurant or someone's house, just say "Shúúh" kind of low as if you're going to say something real serious (it's like saying, "you know what?", your eyebrow raised a bit to indicate disbelief or secrecy). He will turn to you and lean over to share in what will be said. If you call him by name, he may not hear you, but just say "Shúúh" . . ." and his attention is yours for the next hour or so.

He is a cowboy on the side, working at the Pittsburg–Midway mines for a salary. In his younger days, he followed the weekend rodeos—riding sometimes, winning sometimes, and always having a good time. Over the years, younger cowboys came in—they were stronger and faster, taking over the coveted places he and his buddies held for years. These days when he did go to a rodeo, it was to watch and see who was still around. Sometimes he took part in jackpot rodeos nearby during the summers. Now he kept his stock in good shape and rode with his kids now and then. He was glad he had horses and cattle—kept him busy and out of trouble. He met his first wife after high school. She had beautiful long hair. Sometimes he couldn't believe how pretty it was. After all these years, that's all he wanted to remember of her. Not the arguing, fights, or divorce. There were other women, but no one serious. Not even his next wife—she was so young and liked the nightlife. She was a blur in his memory. Only the horses and cattle remained constant through the years. His kids were growing up fast, two already on their own. The younger ones would be gone soon. No longer wanting money or to borrow his pickup.

Lately, he had been trying to remember some of the old stories and songs he had been taught. What were they? The songs to protect the livestock during a winter freeze. And there was one he remembered vaguely to melt the snowdrifts around the corral. He thought that it must be his age—getting older—that made him curious and made him want to hear older Navajos talk. He liked to listen to them discuss things—the way they philosophized was intriguing. They listened to all points of view, not dismissing any, and examined all possibilities of the topic at hand. Sometimes at the trading post he stood near them, listening, and at the same time he looked off into the distance, as if he was waiting for someone. Other times, he helped out at sings and other ceremonies, hauling wood or water; that way he was in the center of everything. He listened, speaking only when necessary, and he observed everything closely. Sometimes he told his children things he had remembered or had just learned, they listened respectfully, and he couldn't tell if it made any impression on them. But to repeat these stories fulfilled something inside him—it was as if he was doing some unspecified duty for himself. When he was alone riding or working, he sang out loud, recalling some songs or making an entirely new song. For now, it seemed his life was good.

When we see him coming toward the house, we say "Ahdii Shúúh," which can mean "Here comes Shúúh," or "Hey, here he comes," or "Listen, he's coming." Right away, you can say to him, "Shúúh, Hágo" then ask him to do something. He's good about that; likes to make himself useful. All good in-laws are supposed to be that way. After we eat, we like to sit around the table and talk for hours and hours. That's how we found out he knows how to talk that old Navajo—the kind we hardly hear anymore. That language is ancient and some words we know the feeling of, but not exactly what they mean. We remember things we were told when we were very young, things we were told as teenagers, and other things we heard just last week. When one person is talking about something, others remember something similar, and then they tell about that. Someone else follows with another memory. We do that—going around the table so that everyone tells about something. Around us, kids run in and out, the screen door slams, coffee cups are refilled, another package of doughnuts appears. Hours pass and finally, one of us will stretch and then we notice the time. Slowly, we get up and attend to other matters. This is when Shúúh starts to leave, shaking hands with everyone and thanking people. He shakes hands with even the littlest kids; they get embarrassed and yet are proud. "Shúúh bił dahdíłghod," we'd say. Shúúh is driving away from here. Someday we will talk about how he didn't know that was his name. That man who really liked stories and was always ready to listen to what you had to talk about.

A Whispered Chant of Loneliness

I awaken at 1:20 then sit in the dark living room.
Numbers click time on silent machines.
Everyone sleeps.
Down the street, music hums, someone laughs.
It floats: an unseen breath through the window screen.

My father uses a cane and each day,
he walks outside to sit in the southern sunlight.
He reads the *National Geographic*, the *Daily Times*,
and the *Gallup Independent*.
He remembers all this and minute details of my life.
Sometimes he tells my children smiling.

His voice is an old rhythm of my childhood.
He read us stories of Goldilocks and The Three Bears
and a pig named "Greased Lightning."
He held us close, sang throaty songs,
and danced Yei bicheii in the kitchen.

His voice is a steady presence in my mothering.
Some years ago, he handed me a cup of coffee
and told me that sometimes leaving a relationship
was an act of abiding strength.
He told me that my children would not be sad always.

Tonight I want to hear him speak to me.
He thinks I look like my mother did at 38.
Just last week, I heard her laughter in my own.

This winter, my life is a series of motions.
Each morning, I get up and shower,
have breakfast for my daughter,
drink a cup of coffee, then warm the car for five minutes.

I continue. My days: an undercurrent of fear,
an outpouring of love,
a whispered chant of loneliness.

Little Pet Stories

Some years back, we had a dog named "Sando—wool" after old man Sandoval, who lived about a mile south of us. My father pronounced his name "Sando-wool" because that was what he called his old friend. Old man Sandoval would ride by our house on his horse, with five or six dogs running alongside. He wore a tall black hat and exchanged silent waves with us. He died long ago. We remember him each time we talk about the pets we have had over the years.

Once my father was at the post office, leaning against the pickup and talking to his buddies, when a little straggly kitten crept around the corner. He picked it up and examined it. He put it in the pickup like it was his, then brought it home for us. We fed it, bathed it, and named it "Polly." Polly stayed with us for years and had many kittens. She was a pretty calico, and for a long time, we were able to trace her offspring through the many relatives and families who took kittens of hers.

Once my father and brothers were digging postholes for a chaha'oh, a summer shade house. Then my brother stopped suddenly because there was an open hole underground where he was digging. He called us and we looked inside and there were several tiny baby rabbits. My mother's pet, Anna, had babies earlier that day. We were amazed at how small and pink the babies were. Their fur was thin and transparent. Carefully, my brother lifted them out and we wrapped them in handkerchiefs in Anna's hutch. We watched them until Anna came hopping back and immediately, they nuzzled into her long fur, sensing warmth and safety. The men decided to move the chaha'oh over a few yards, in case there were other homes they couldn't see.

The Motion of Songs Rising

The October night is warm and clear.
We are standing on a small hill and in all directions,
around us, the flat land listens to the songs rising.
The holy ones are here dancing.
The Yeis are here.

In the west, Shiprock looms above the desert.
Tsé bit'a'í, old bird-shaped rock. She watches us.
Tsé bit'a'í, our mother who brought the people here on her back.
Our refuge from the floods long ago. It was worlds and centuries ago,
yet she remains here. Nihimá, our mother

This is the center of the night
and right in front of us, the holy ones dance.
They dance, surrounded by hundreds of Navajos.

> Diné t'óó àhayói.
> Diné t'óó àhayói.

We listen and watch the holy ones dance.

> Yeibicheii.
> Ycibichcii.
> Grandfather of the holy ones.

They dance, moving back and forth.
Their bodies are covered with white clay
and they wave evergreen branches.
They wear hides of varying colors,
their coyote tails swinging as they sway back and forth.
All of them dancing ancient steps.
They dance precise steps, our own emergence onto this land.

They dance again, the formation of this world.
They dance for us now—one precise swaying motion.
They dance back and forth, back and forth.
As they are singing, we watch ourselves recreated.

Éí áłts'íísígíí shił nizhóní. The little clown must be about six years
old. He skips lightly about waving his branches around. He teases
people in the audience, tickling their faces if they look too serious or
too sleepy. At the beginning of each dance, when the woman walks by to
bless the Yeis, he runs from her. Finally, after the third time, she
sprinkles him with corn pollen and he skips off happily. 'éí shił nizhóní.

The Yeis are dancing again, each step, our own strong bodies.
They are dancing the same dance, thousands of years old. They are here
for us now, grateful for another harvest and our own good health.
> The roasted corn I had this morning was fresh,
> cooked all night and taken out of the ground this
> morning. It was steamed and browned just right.

They are dancing and in the motion of songs rising,
our breathing becomes the morning moonlit air.
The fires are burning below as always.
> We are restored.
> We are restored.

Uncle's Journey

Natalie lived in the north valley of Albuquerque and in her neighborhood, there were small ditches, old adobe homes, and lots of big, tree-lined places to explore. Natalie was in first grade and had an older sister and brother.

One day a lot of her relatives, from the Navajo reservation far away, came to Natalie's house in the city. She knew some of them, but there were some relatives she didn't know, or didn't remember. They remembered Natalie, though, and said she had grown so much. Natalie helped serve coffee and set the table. Her Grandma and Grandpa came also, and they hugged and held her for a long time.

Natalie noticed that everyone was quiet and sometimes it seemed that they might cry. While people ate, the adults began to talk and Natalie sat and listened. It was then that she understood the sadness in the house. Her Uncle Jerry, her mother's brother, was very sick.

Natalie was surprised because the last time Uncle Jerry had come to visit, he looked well and had played with her.

"Mama," she said. "Uncle wasn't sick the last time, remember?"

"No," her mother said. "They just found out yesterday, shi awéé', my baby, a little blood cell turned white inside him and now it's growing bigger. It's called "cancer." It makes him feel sick, my baby."

Natalie, her family, and all her relatives went to the hospital to see Uncle Jerry. Everyone over fourteen was allowed to visit him. Natalie and the other children played outside on the grass. Uncle was on the third floor and once in a while, he waved at them from the window. They could see his wheelchair.

"Uncle! Shidá'í!" they yelled when they saw him at the window. Later they sent him messages and notes, and when he felt okay, he wrote back. Natalie's mother said that their drawings and cards were taped on the walls in his room. Once they wrote him a note, saying,

"Do you like hospital food?"

He wrote back, "Yuk! Save me." They laughed and laughed.

A few days later, some relatives from Rock Point went back for a few days. Others from Fort Defiance came to the hospital. Their homes were so far away that when Natalie's family went there, she slept most of the way. Some of her aunts had campers on their pickups and they stayed in the hospital parking lot. When Natalie felt sleepy at the hospital, she took a nap in one of the campers. They stayed at the hospital most of the time and there were lots of people at their house. She wasn't lonely anymore. Before this, she had complained to her mother about having no one to play with. Now she had a lot of brothers and sisters to play with. In Navajo, there isn't another way to say "cousins." Natalie showed them the ditches and they climbed trees and played baseball in the vacant lots.

After a few months, Uncle Jerry felt better and most of the relatives went back to their reservation homes. Uncle spent the weekends at Natalie's house. Natalie's mother was happy and she baked fudge marble cake all the time. It was Uncle's favorite. Her mother laughed a lot and told stories about when she and Uncle were little children.

Natalie pushed Uncle around in his wheelchair and brought him water and the newspaper. In the evenings, they sat outside on the porch after supper. Sometimes they played catch and once when they were telling stories, Natalie fell asleep beside his wheelchair. When someone laughed, she opened her eyes, and the sky was full of stars. They sparkled and glimmered so. She crawled onto Uncle's lap and he said,

"See the stars, Natalie? They take care of you. They're your relatives. They see everything and everybody. Your Grandpa who died is up there. Don't be afraid at night, because the stars watch you, baby."

Natalie fell asleep again.

Soon Uncle went back into the hospital, and school began. Her family had spent most of the summer at the hospital with him. Now he had become sicker. Most of their relatives returned to the city and their children watched the window, in case he looked out. Some days, Natalie went to school straight from the hospital. They drew pictures for Uncle and finally, the hospital allowed all the children to go into his room. Uncle was still and slept all the time. Natalie held his fingers and cried. The doctor had told her mother that he might not get well.

In his room, the children invented games to play and told scary stories about the nurses. They told each other that if kids didn't smile at a nurse, the nurses would use that as a reason to give the kid a shot. Then they hid when the nurses came into the room. They played quietly because they could not be noisy. Natalie's mother and aunts sat and talked quietly among themselves. They cried a lot and their eyes stayed red and puffy.

Natalie stayed by her Grandpa most of the time. He was old and hardly spoke at all. She brought him water and put his cane in a safe place so it wouldn't get lost. Uncle was Grandpa's youngest child. There wasn't anything that Grandpa could do for Uncle Jerry. Natalie knew that there wasn't anything anyone could do. And so she stayed by Grandpa.

Winter came and Uncle hardly woke anymore. He slept, breathing loudly, and when he moaned, everyone would look at him and then at each other. Natalie didn't feel like playing anymore, and she was sleepy all the time. Sometimes someone read to the children or told them stories.

They prayed and cried when the big people started to cry. Natalie's brother was fourteen and the oldest of the nieces and nephews. He held a meeting for the children, like the adults did, and told them to hold hands and pray.

"Uncle is going to die," he said, "and it's really sad for our Moms and Dads. They'll never see their younger brother again. It's up to us kids to take care of them, to help them, and to be good."

He told them not to fight and fuss with each other. He told them to help take care of the babies. After Uncle died, he would be traveling for four days to the next world, he said, and everything they did during that time would be for him. They would have to eat all their food to give Uncle strength for his journey. They listened and cried for Uncle and themselves.

A few days later, Natalie was sleeping on an empty bed in Uncle's room when suddenly someone yelled out loud and they rushed to his bed. He was quiet. The loud breathing had stopped. Natalie looked at the clock and both hands were on four—that she remembered for a long time. Uncle Jerry died on Tuesday evening. Natalie cried out loud and ran to hold her mother, then to her father, her aunts, her Grandma, and to her sisters and brothers. Everyone was crying and holding each other. Natalie stayed by her Grandpa for a long time.

Then the doctor came in and pulled the curtain around Uncle's bed. They left the hospital slowly, holding onto each other. The nurses were crying by the elevators.

Everyone went to Natalie's house. Even though the house was crowded, it was quiet as they held a meeting to plan for the next four days.

That night all the relatives left the city. The sky was cloudy. Natalie helped pack clothes, bedding, and food for the family. It was 200 miles to Grandma's house and everything would be closed along the way. They locked the house and left the city. They drove without stopping for a long time. The sky was white and cloudy.

Natalie kept falling asleep. Whenever she woke, her parents were talking and crying softly. Natalie knew how far they still had to travel by the smooth cliffs near Laguna, the mountains at Tohatchi, and the flat desert by Newcomb.

It began to snow. The snow fell in large flakes and soon it was as if they were driving in a white soundless world. They were all alone on the highway and couldn't see any hills or mountains. Natalie kept asking, "Where are we? Are we almost there?" Even though she already knew the answers.

Soon all of them were quiet. The pickup was sliding and her father couldn't see the road. Natalie said, "Good thing, Uncle is already at Shiprock." Her brother had told her that the hospital had already flown him back and it had only taken forty minutes. It was taking them over five hours because of the snow.

Near Table Mesa, the storm broke. The highway was still snow-packed and icy. But the sky cleared and the stars sparkled. Natalie knew then that they would be safe and wouldn't slide off the road. "Uncle is watching us," Natalie said. "He's a star now, Mama."

The next four days were sad and everyone tried to do things in the right way. They didn't go to basketball games or to movies in town. They understood that the family needed to stay together while Uncle was traveling. The children helped serve and cook food and kept the wood and coal boxes full all day. They met many of Uncle's friends and listened to the stories they told about him. They ate everything that was served so that Uncle would have strength for his journey. Several times during the four days, different people stood and spoke to everyone. The speakers gave advice and said that all families should help each other and learn the way things have always been done. Everyone prayed for Uncle Jerry, Grandma and Grandpa, and all of the family and relatives.

When the four days were over, they knew Uncle had arrived at the next world. They told stories and although they missed him, they tried not to cry too much. And on clear nights when Natalie went out on the back porch, there was Uncle Jerry—bright and sparkling.

The Snakeman

The child slid down silently and caught herself at the end of the fire escape. She eased herself down until she felt the cold, hard sidewalk through her slippers, then let go.

The night was clear and quiet. The only noise that could be heard was the echo of the child's footsteps in the moonlit alley behind the old brick buildings.

The little girls, watching her from the top floor of the dorm, swung the window screen in and out, catching it before it struck the window frame. They always talked about what would happen if the top hinges suddenly gave way, but they hadn't yet.

"Good thing it's spring," one of them said

"She would freeze her toes off for sure," another answered.

"Shhh!" the biggest one hissed.

They whispered in lispy voices and someone on the other side of the room would only hear, "Ss . . . ss," hissing, and an occasional "Shut up!" The room was large with windows on three sides. The fire escape the child slid down was in the center of the north windows, which faced a big dark hill, its slope covered with huge round rocks and dry tumbleweeds.

Sometimes the dorm mother, who lived at the other end of the hall, would hear them giggling or running around. She would walk down the dark, shiny hall so fast that her housecoat would fly out behind her in billows. The girls would scurry to their beds, tripping over their long nightgowns, finally faking snores as she turned on the harsh, bright lights in each room. After she went back to her room, the children jumped up and down and laughed silently with wide, open mouths, and pounded little fists into their beds.

One of the girls whispered loudly, "She's coming back!" They all ran noiselessly to the window and watched the small figure coming. The little girl walked briskly with her hands in her housecoat pockets.

She wore the soft wool slippers all the girls made for their sisters or mothers at Christmas. She didn't have sisters or a mother, so she wore them herself.

"Seems like she floats," one girl commented.

"How could she? Can't you hear her walking?" the biggest retorted.

The girls went back to their beds, and the ones closest to the fire escape opened the window and held it up until she was in. Then they all gathered at one bed and sat in the moonlight telling ghost stories or about how the end of the world was *really* going to be. Except for the girl who walked. She was quiet and always went right to sleep when she returned.

Sometimes late at night or toward morning when the sun hadn't come up completely, everything was quiet and the room filled with the soft, even breathing of the children; one of them might stand at the window facing east and think of home far away, tears streaming down her face. Late in the night, someone always cried, and if the others heard her, they pretended not to notice. They understood how it was with all of them—if only they could go to public school and eat at home everyday.

In the morning before they went downstairs to dress, two girls would empty their pockets of small torn pieces of paper and scatter them under the beds. The beds had white ruffled bed skirts that reached the floor and the paper bits weren't visible unless the bed skirt was lifted. This was how they tested the girl who swept their room. In the evenings, they checked under the beds to see if the paper was gone. If it wasn't, they immediately reported it to the dorm mother, who didn't ask how they were so sure their room hadn't been cleaned.

The building was divided into three floors and an attic. The youngest girls, who were in grade school, occupied the top and bottom floors, and the junior high girls had the middle floor. The bedrooms were on the top floor and all daytime activity took place on the bottom floor. The building was old, like all other buildings on campus, and the students were sure that the buildings were haunted. How could it not be? they asked among themselves. This was especially true for the little girls in the north end of the dorm because they were so close to the attic door. There was a man in there, they said in hushed voices, who kept the attic door open just a little, enough to throw evil powder on anyone who walked by. For this reason, they kept out of the hallway at night.

Once they had heard him coming down the stairs to the hallway door and the smaller girls started crying. They all slept two to a bed, and the bigger girls made sure all the little ones had someone bigger with them. They stayed up later than usual, crying and praying. No one woke early enough to get everyone back to their own beds, and the dorm mother had spanked all of them. It was okay because nothing had happened to any of them that night, they said.

Once when the little girl went on one of her walks, the others were waiting for her as usual. Two girls were trying to figure out how to get to the bathroom down the hall when they heard scratching noises outside on the sidewalk.

"You guys! Come here! He's over here!" they whispered loudly. They ran to the west window and saw a dark figure go around the corner, and the biggest girl took control.

"You two get over by that window. You, on that side. Someone get on the fire escape, in case he tries to come up here."

They watched the man below and tried to get a description of him, in case someone asked them. They couldn't see him very well because he was on the shaded side of the building. Some of the girls started crying and others crawled quietly back into bed. Two of the bigger girls waited to open the window for the other girl. When she came back, they huddled around her and told her, crying a little. She said he was probably a father trying to see his daughter and maybe the mother won't let him see her. Then the girls calmed down and tried to figure out whose parents were divorced or argued a lot. They finally decided that he was the boyfriend of a junior high girl downstairs.

When a new girl came, she asked why the girl always walked at night and the biggest one had answered,

"Wouldn't you if you could see your mother every night, dummy?"

"Well, where's her mom? Can't she see her on weekends like us? That's not fair."

"Fair? *Fair?*" they had all yelled in disbelief.

Then the girl who walked explained that her parents had died years ago when she was six and that they were buried at the school cemetery. That's why she walked over to see them. Although she saw her mother more.

"How is she? Can she talk?"

"Can you really see her?" the new girl asked.

"Yeah," she answered patiently. "She calls me and waits at the edge of the cemetery by those small fat trees. She's real pretty. When she died, they put a blue outfit on her. A Navajo skirt that's real long, and a shiny, soft blouse. She waves at me like this, 'Come here, shiyázhí, my little one.' She always calls me that. She's soft and smells so good."

The girls nodded, each remembering their own mothers.

"When it's cold or snowing, I stand inside her blanket with her. We talk about when I was a baby or what I'll do when I grow up. She always worries about if I'm being good or not."

"Mine, too," someone murmured.

"Why do mothers always want their kids to be goody-good?"

"So you won't die at the end of the world, dummy!"

"Dying isn't that bad. You can still visit people like her mom does."

"But at the end of the world, all the dinosaurs and monsters that are sleeping in the mountains will bust out and eat all the bad people. No one can escape, either," said the oldest girl with confidence.

Then the little girl who talked to her mother every night said quietly, "No one can be that bad." She went to her bed and lay there looking at the ceiling until she fell asleep. The other girls gathered on two beds and sat in a circle and talked in tight, little voices about the snakeman who sometimes stole jewelry from them.

"You can't see him," one said, " 'cause he's like a blur that moves real fast and you just see a black thing go by."

"He has a silver bracelet, and if he shines it on you, you're a goner 'cause it paralyzes."

They talked until they began looking around to make sure he wasn't in the room. The bigger girls slept with the little ones, and they prayed together that God wouldn't let the man in the attic or the snakeman come to them. They prayed that the world wouldn't end before their parents came to visit.

As the room became quiet and the breathing even and soft, the little girl got up, put on her housecoat, and slid soundlessly down the fire escape.

What I Am

Nineteen hundred thirty-five. Kinłichíi'nii Bitsí waited, looking across the snow-covered desert stretching out before her. Snow was falling lightly and the desert was flat and white. From where she stood at the foothills of the Carriso Mountains, she could see for miles.

She would see him when he approached—a small, dark speck on the vast whiteness, moving slowly, but closer. Her son, Prettyboy, tall and lanky on the surefooted horse. She would see him.

All evening, she kept watch, stepping out every once in a while. He had gone to visit some relatives at Little Shiprock and should have returned by now. It had begun snowing early and continued into the evening. She knew Prettyboy had started home before the storm and would be arriving soon. She kept watch, looking out on the horizon.

In those days, hogans had no windows so she stood at the front door, a shawl around her shoulders. Only her eyes were uncovered as she squinted, looking out into the desert night. "Nihimá, deesk'aaz. Our mother, it's cold," her children called her inside. She would come in for a while, then go back out to watch for him again. All evening she waited, and her children urged her not to worry. He would be home soon they said. She continued watching for him, insisting that she wasn't cold.

Finally, she saw him, a dark speck on the horizon. She rushed in and stirred up the fire, heated up the stew, and put on a fresh pot of coffee. She heated up the grease for frybread. He came in, damp and cold with snow. They laughed because his eyebrows were frozen white. "Tell us everything about your trip," they said to him. "Tell us about your trip." While he ate, he talked about the relatives he visited and the news that he had heard. He said the horse seemed to know the way by itself through the snow and wind. He kept his head down most of the way, he said. The snow was blowing and it was hard to see. The family finally went to bed, relieved that Prettyboy was safely home. Outside the wind blew and the snow formed drifts around the hogan.

In the morning, Kinłichíi'nii Bitsí was sick—feverish and dizzy. She didn't get up and they fed her blue corn mush and weak Navajo tea to drink. She slept most of the day and felt very warm. Her family began to worry. The nearest medical doctor was in Shiprock, fifty miles to the east. On horseback, it was a full day's journey. Even then, the doctor was at the agency only two days a week, and they couldn't remember which days he was there. A medicineman lived nearby on the mountainside, and they decided to wait until morning to go over there and alert him, if they had to. She would get better, they said, and they prayed and sang songs for strength and for the children. Very late that night, she became very ill and talked incessantly about her children and grandchildren.

She died before morning, and Prettyboy went out into the snow and blowing wind to tell other relatives who lived at distances from the hogan of Kinłichíi'nii Bitsí. People gathered quickly despite the snow; they came from all around to help out with the next four days.

Nineteen hundred sixty-eight. The granddaughter of Kinłichíi'nii Bitsí said:

My Uncle Prettyboy died today, and we went over to his house. His aunt, my grandma, was sweeping out her hogan next door and scolding the young people for not helping out. They were listening to the radios in their pickups and holding hands. You know, they are teenagers. My grandma is 104 years old. My real grandma, Kinłichíi'nii Bitsí, would have been 106 if she hadn't died in the 1930s. I know a lot about her through stories they told me. I know how she was. I think I'm like her in some ways.

At Prettyboy's house, his wife and children were sitting in the front room, and people came in and spoke to them quietly. They were crying and crying; sometimes loudly, sometimes sobbing. In the kitchen, and outside over open fires, we were cooking and preparing food for everyone who had come following his death.

Prettyboy was a tall man and he died of cancer. It was awful because he didn't even smoke. But he had worked in the uranium mines near Red Valley, like many other Navajo men, and was exposed to radioactive materials.

Last week when we were hoeing in the field, my mother told me, "Having a mother is everything. Your mother is your home. When children come home, the mother is always ready with food, stories, and songs for the little ones. She's always happy to see her children and grandchildren."

She had always told me this as I was growing up. That day when we were hoeing corn, I asked her, "Tell me about my grandmother and how you knew something was wrong that time. Tell me the story, shima."

She told me, saying.

That night Prettyboy was coming home, I knew something was wrong. The wind blew hard and roared through the tall pine trees. We lived in the mountains at Oak Springs, ten miles above where my mother lived. We were just married then. Our first baby, your oldest sister, was a month old.

That night the dogs started barking wildly and loudly; they were afraid of something. Then they stopped suddenly. Your father and I looked at each other across the room. Then we heard the coyotes barking and yelping outside. He opened the door and they were circling the hogan, running around and around, yelping the whole time. Your father grabbed the rifle and shot at the coyotes, but he missed each time. He missed. He had been a sharpshooter in the army, and he couldn't shoot them. Finally, they ran off, and we were both afraid. We talked and prayed into the night. We couldn't go anywhere. The snow was deep, and even the horses would have a hard time.

In the morning, I went out to pray and I saw my brother, Prettyboy, riding up to our hogan. He was still far away, but even then, I knew something had happened. I tried not to cry, but I knew in my bones something had happened. My brother would not ride out in that weather just to visit. Even though the sun was out, the snow was frozen, and the wind blew steadily. I held the baby and prayed, hoping I was wrong.

Finally, as he came up to our hogan, I went out and I could see that he was crying. He wasn't watching where he was going. The horse led my brother who was crying. I watched him, and then he saw me. I called out, "Shínaaí, my older brother!" He got off the horse and ran to me, crying out, "Shideezhí, nihimá adin. My younger sister, our mother's gone!" My heart fell. We cried. The wind stopped blowing and we went inside.

I held my baby girl and told her she would not see her grandmother. Neither would our other children. My mother died, and I realized that she was my home. She had always welcomed us, and since I was the youngest, she called me "baby." "Even if you are a grandmother, you will be my baby always," she often said to me.

When my mother told this story, we always cried. Even if I had known Kinłichíi'nii Bitsí, I couldn't love her more than I do now— knowing her only through stories and my mother's memory.

My grandmother had talked to my father about a week before she died. She told him, "Take care of her. She is my youngest, my baby. I trust you, and I have faith that you will care for her as I have all these years. She is my baby, but she knows what to do. Listen to her and remember that a woman's wisdom is not foolish. She knows a lot, because I have raised her to be a good and kind person."

My father listened, and he treats my mother well. He listens to her and abides by her wishes.

Nineteen hundred eighty-seven. The great-granddaughter of Kinłichíi'nii Bitsí said:

Early in the morning, we went out to pray. The corn pollen drifted into the swimming pool, becoming little specks of yellow on the blue water. The water lapped quietly against the edges. We prayed and asked the holy ones and my ancestors who died before to watch over me.

I was going so far away to Europe. What a trip it would be. My grandma called the evening before I left and said, "Remember who you are. You're from Oak Springs, and all your relatives are thinking about you and praying that you will come back safely. Do well on your trip, my little one." I was nervous and couldn't sleep. I felt like changing my mind, but my mother had already spent all that money. She promised she wouldn't cry at the airport, then she did. I know that my little sister teased her about it.

I put the bag of pollen in my purse. At La Guardia Airport, I went to the bathroom and tasted some. My mother, I thought, my grandmother, help me. Everything was confusing and loud, so many people smoking and talking loudly. I wanted my mother's soft, slow voice more than anything. I was the only Indian in the group, and no one knew how I felt. The other girls were looking at boys and giggling.

At least I had the corn pollen. I was afraid they would arrest me at customs for carrying an unknown substance, but they didn't. I knew I was meant to go to Paris.

I prayed on top of the Eiffel Tower, and the pollen floated down to the brick plaza below. I was so far away from home, so far above everything. The tower swayed a bit in the wind. I never missed Indians until I went abroad. I was lonely to see an Indian the whole time. People thought I was "neat"—being a "real" Indian. They asked all kinds of questions and wanted to learn Navajo. It was weird to be a "real" Indian. All along, I was just regular, one of the bunch, laughing with relatives and friends, mixing Navajo and English. We were always telling jokes about cowboys, computer warriors, and stuff.

It was while I stood on top of the Eiffel Tower that I understood that who I am is my mother, her mother, and my great-grandmother, Kinłichíi'nii Bitsí. It was she who made sure I got through customs and wasn't mugged in Paris. When I returned, my grandmother was at the airport. She hugged me tightly. My mother stood back, then came forward and held me. I was home.

Acknowledgments

The works in this volume that have appeared in other publications are acknowledged as follows:

POEMS

"Blue Horses Rush In," *Frontiers: A Journal of Women Studies* 12 (3): 167–70, 1992.

"In 1864," *Frontiers: A Journal of Women Studies* 12 (3): 1–4, 1992.

"It Was a Special Treat," first published in *The Remembered Earth* (Albuquerque: Red Earth Press, 1978), p. 306.

"It Has Always Been This Way," *Dine Be'iina: A Journal of Navajo Life* 2 (1): 84, 86, (Shiprock, New Mexico: Navajo Community College, 1990).

"Leda and the Cowboy," *Frontiers: A Journal of Women Studies* 12 (3): 165–66, 1992.

"These Long Drives," *Dine Be'iina: A Journal of Navajo Life* 2 (1): 83–84, 1990. Appeared under the title "How I Miss My Brothers Tonight."

"Hills Brothers Coffee," first published in *The Remembered Earth* (Albuquerque: Red Earth Press, 1978), p. 307.

"Dit'oodi": *Bombay Gin* (Boulder, Colorado: The Naropa Institute, 1990), pp. 31–32.

"Raisin Eyes," first published in *Seasonal Woman* (Santa Fe: Tooth of Time Press, 1981), pp. 40–41.

"What Danger We Court," first published in *Caliban* 5:100, Ann Arbor, 1988.

"It Is Night in Oklahoma," *Guadalupe Review* 1:100–101, San Antonio, 1991.

STORIES

"The Snakeman," first published in *Sun Tracks*, University of Arizona, 1978, pp. 11–12, and *The Remembered Earth* (Albuquerque: Red Earth Press, 1978), pp. 308–310.

"What I Am," first published in *Recent Ones That Are Made* (Santa Fe: Wheelwright Museum, 1988), pp. 37–39, and *Sonora Review* 14–15:55–58, University of Arizona, 1988.

About the Author

LUCI TAPAHONSO was born and raised in Shiprock, New Mexico, and is a member of the Navajo Nation. She is an assistant professor of English at the University of Kansas in Lawrence, Kansas, where she lives with her husband and children. She has published three books of poetry, *One More Shiprock Night*, *Seasonal Woman*, and *A Breeze Swept Through* and has been published in numerous journals and anthologies. Her poetry has been featured in several national radio and television programs, such as National Public Radio's "New Letters."